*The authors would like to dedicate this
book to the inventors of the toilet flush, without
whom we'd still be using buckets of water – yuck!*

First published 2008 by Walker Books Ltd
87 Vauxhall Walk, London SE11 5HJ

4 6 8 10 9 7 5

© 2008 Duncan McCoshan and Jem Packer

The right of Duncan McCoshan and Jem Packer to be identified
as author/illustrator of this work has been asserted by them
in accordance with the Copyright, Designs and Patents Act 1988

This book has been typeset in Shinn Light

Printed in the UK by Clays Ltd, St Ives plc

British Library Cataloguing in Publication Data:
a catalogue record for this book is available
from the British Library

ISBN 978-1-4063-0306-3

www.walker.co.uk

But before we get to the gross stuff let's meet our heroes, **Gerald**, **Gene** and **Fleabag Monkeyface**. Here's a few things you need to know about them:

Gene
Likes: Making lists, especially of gross things
Dislikes: Bunny rabbits
Favourite word: "Unreal"
You should know: Gene has the ideas

Gerald
Likes: The sound of a toilet flushing
Dislikes: Clean towels
Favourite word: "Cool"
You should know: Gerald has the stupid habit of liking Gene's ideas

Fleabag Monkeyface
Likes: Eating nits
Dislikes: Baths, showers and soap
Favourite word: "Ug-brilliant"
You should know: He's got Gross-Out Power

Without Gerald, Gene and Fleabag the world would be a much cleaner, shinier place.

But let's start at the beginning...

1 It was a lovely sunny day, the sort of day when you might expect kids to head to the park or a funfair. But Gerald, Gene and Fleabag Monkeyface were going somewhere much more exciting – well, to them anyway. They were going to the town's **sewage treatment plant**!

"I can't wait to film the huge stinking piles of yuckiness," said Gene. "Unreal!"

"And what about where they filter out the horrible bits?" said Gerald. "Cool!"

"I'd like to ug-move in," said Fleabag. "Ug-brilliant!"

In fact Gerald, Gene and Fleabag loved all things gross. And their love of grossness was always getting them into trouble!

Gerald once dropped a set of his grandmother's false teeth into the school dinner.

At a school football match **Gene** once put a slug in the goalie's gloves.

And **Fleabag Monkeyface** once served up a banana split that was twelve years past its sell-by date!

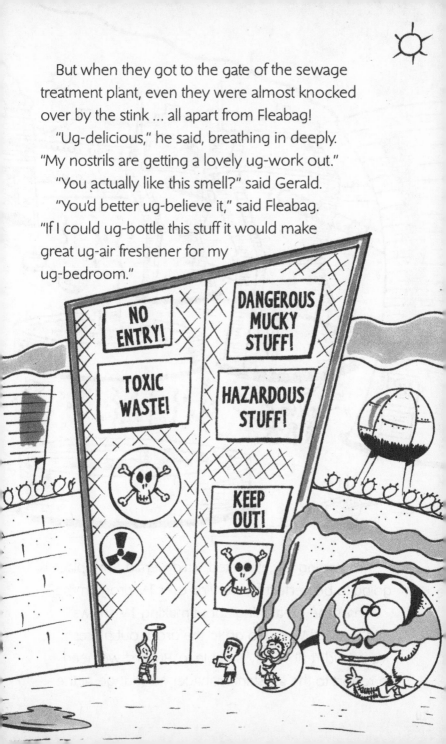

But when they got to the gate of the sewage treatment plant, even they were almost knocked over by the stink ... all apart from Fleabag!

"Ug-delicious," he said, breathing in deeply. "My nostrils are getting a lovely ug-work out."

"You actually like this smell?" said Gerald.

"You'd better ug-believe it," said Fleabag. "If I could ug-bottle this stuff it would make great ug-air freshener for my ug-bedroom."

NO ENTRY!

DANGEROUS MUCKY STUFF!

TOXIC WASTE!

HAZARDOUS STUFF!

KEEP OUT!

"I'm starting to get excited," said Gerald. "This place is going to be perfect for our first-ever TV programme."

"That's the great thing about making TV shows," said Gene. "We get to go to the gross-out places we wouldn't normally be able to. But first we need to report to the assistant manager, Mr Plunge, at the main office – he's going to show us round."

They walked past pools of frothing
muck and bubbling ponds of filth.

"This is going to be great!"
said Gerald as they reached
the door of the office.

2 But Gerald, Gene and Fleabag were about to get a shock that was going to wobble them to the tips of their toes.

EMPLOYEE OF THE MONTH

MATT SHINE

WELCOME TO
Sweetwater
Sewage
Treatment
Plant
THE YUCK STOPS HERE

FLUSHING NEWS

Sweetwater Sewage
Treatment Plant
AWARD-WINNING SCALE MODEL

There in the reception area were Gerald, Gene and Fleabag's arch-rivals and next-door neighbours, the **Smugley twins**. As usual these lovers of all things cuddly were with their pets, **Lamby** and **Wamby**.

"Why are they here?!" whispered Gerald.

"In a sewage plant?!" said Gene.

"And I was having such an ug-brilliant ug-day!" said Fleabag.

"**Euuuuuuak!**" screeched Mandy Smugley.
"What are *you* doing here?"

"We've come to film the sewage works for
Gross-Out TV," said Gene.

"Who would want to see that? Now get away from
Lamby and Wamby," wheedled Randy Smugley. "Our
lovely little lambs are allergic to dirtiness and your
monkey friend looks even more rancid than usual."

"What about you?" asked Gerald. "A sewage plant
is the last place we'd expect to find you."

"Daddy is the general manager," said Mandy proudly.

"And Mummy has brought us here to give him his packed lunch," added Randy.

"His favourite," said the Smugley twins' mother, Brandy Smugley...

Mrs Smugley's "How To Make a Perfect Sandwich"

1 Procure the fluffiest white cheesy bread. Add symmetrical rectangles of ham.

2 Utilize a scalpel for micro-thin slivers of tomato.

3 AVOID messy mayonnaise. Mummify in clingfilm - yum!

PERFECT SANDWICH

Just then the door opened...

As soon as Mr Smugley entered the room Gerald, Gene and Fleabag could see the family resemblance.

"Hello, I'm Andy Smugley. But you can call me **Mr Smugley**, or **sir**." He shook Gerald's hand then produced an antiseptic wipe and scrubbed his hand. Then he shook Gene's hand and once again cleaned his hand.

"I get through a pack a day," he chuckled nervously. But when he reached Fleabag, he turned pale and did not hold out his hand.

"What is this?" he asked, looking disgusted. "I am not sure if my hand wipes will be strong enough. We could put you through one of our industrial cleaners..."

"That won't be ug-necessary," said Fleabag, who was starting to think Mr Smugley was as unpleasant as his kids.

"Unfortunately, Mr Plunge, who was meant to show you round, is off sick," said Mr Smugley. "So I'm going to have to take you on the tour."

"Great!" said Gene. "We want to see the most disgusting bits so we can film them."

"Disgusting bits?" said Mr Smugley, scrunching up his nose. "I usually like to stay in the office and avoid the disgusting bits. You see, what I like about managing a sewage treatment plant is that I get to make dirty things clean."

NORTH, SOUTH, EAST, WEST
✦✦✦✦✦✦✦✦
CLEAN, CLEAN, CLEAN IS BEST!

Certificate of Honours Degree in Sludge Management Sparklee College

MR A. SMUGLEY, MANAGER

With his family safe in the nice clean office, Mr Smugley reluctantly began showing Gerald, Gene and Fleabag around the sewage treatment plant. Although he seemed totally revolted by what he was showing them, the crew of Gross-Out TV were loving it! With the cameras rolling, their first-ever programme was now in production.

"Firstly, we have an initial **screening** of litter and **de-gritting** of crude sewage," said Mr Smugley, wiping his hands with an antiseptic wipe, which he did every time he opened a door or gate.

"Crude ug-sewage?" asked Fleabag.

"Use your imagination," said Gene. Not even *he* wanted to get into the details of that.

"Is there an ug-gift shop?" asked Fleabag. "It would be ug-great if you did an ug-pick-and-ug-mix!" But Mr Smugley pretended not to hear him and carried on with the tour.

"The screening happens in these large tanks and takes about two hours," he said, turning a little green. "I'm not feeling very well, let's press on."

"The second stage is called **aeration**," he continued. "This is where air is bubbled through the settled sewage to encourage the growth of micro-organisms."

"Micro-organisms?" asked Gerald.

"Yes, dey reduce de dreatment load and abonia during a four-hour process," said Mr Smugley, holding his nose.

*"De resultant microbial soub is called **actibated sludge**."*

"I like ug-soup!" said Fleabag, pulling out a spoon from his trouser pocket. "And I am ug-hungry!"

"I think we should wait until lunch," said Gene.

19

"Phew," said Mr Smugley, releasing his nose. "That's the worst bit over. The last treatment stage is called **'final settlement'**. Here the activated sludge settles in tanks to leave a clean effluent to flow out to the river. Now, if you'll excuse me, I must get back to my office – I'm in urgent need of clean air."

"And what's in here?" asked Gene, who had noticed a large vat in a fenced-off area bristling with barbed wire and toxic warning signs.

"Oh, you can't go in there," said Mr Smugley. "That vat contains some of the most unpleasant material we have to deal with – **zoo poo**."

"Zoo poo?" asked Gene. "What's that?"

"It's waste that comes from the town zoo," said Mr Smugley.

"You mean like baboon droppings and gazelle pee?" said Gerald.

"Well, it's from one animal in particular," said Mr Smugley. "Ever since the zoo acquired Gargantua the gorilla, the waste has been exceedingly volatile – which is why we have to take these safety measures."

But Fleabag had heard enough. He jumped into the forbidden area to get a closer look at the metal container.

"I've got to ug-check this ug-stuff out," said Fleabag as he tugged on the stopper. "Ug-gorilla waste – this is the ug-chance of an ug-lifetime!"

"Get your ape away from that!" screeched Mr Smugley. "It's highly toxic!"

But it was too late – Fleabag had tugged out the stopper.

"Oh no!" screamed Mr Smugley. "It's leaking into the aeration tank!"

As the putrid substance leaked into the tank, the mixture started to bubble and boil.

"Ug-yikes!" said Fleabag.

"I think we should get away nooooooooooooow!" screeched Mr Smugley. But it was too late and there was a huge...

4 The entire contents of the sludge pool had been blown into the air ... and was heading back towards the ground – fast!

"We need to get out of here *quickly!*" shrieked Mr Smugley. "Or we'll all be buried alive in microbial soup!"

"Fleabag, time for **Gross-Out Power**," said Gene.

"And quickly!" added Gerald.

Fleabag scrunched up his face, then scooped up Gerald and Gene. But Mr Smugley batted him away, preferring to face the sludge on his own.

"Ug-supersonic sneeze alert!" shouted Fleabag as he unleashed a ground-shattering sneeze.

The power of the sneeze was so great that the three of them were blasted out of the sewage plant and into the car park.

AAATCHOOO!

Just as they landed the contents of the sludge pool splattered down on the plant.

"That was an ug-close one," said Fleabag. "Although I would have quite ug-liked to have had an ug-shower in microbial ug-soup."

"Phew!" said Gene.

"You saved us from a sludging!" said Gerald.

But not everyone had been so lucky. When they heard the explosion Mrs Smugley, Randy and Mandy had come out to see what was going on and, along with Mr Smugley, were now covered in muck...

"My babies!" squealed Mr Smugley, looking at his filthy wife and children. "The tour is over," he barked over the wall at Gerald, Gene and Fleabag. "Don't even think of coming back in here. I'll be sending your parents a bill for clearing this lot up..."

Gerald, Gene and Fleabag decided it was best not to hang around, and left the sewage treatment plant in a hurry. But as they left Gene made a terrible discovery.

"Oh no!" he said. "Our film equipment – it's ruined!" Although they had avoided the sludge, their camera and microphone hadn't been so lucky.

"All that footage of a sludge explosion – gone!" said Gerald.

"We'll always have our ug-memories," chuckled Fleabag. "That's one of the funniest ug-sights I've ever ug-seen!"

6 But as soon as Gerald, Gene and Fleabag left some strange things began to happen at the sewage plant...

All four Smugleys were now covered in the sludge, but this was not any old sludge. A chemical reaction had happened during the explosion. It was now **TOXIC SLUDGE** – and it was having some remarkable side effects.

"My precious darlings!" squealed Mr Smugley, who could barely move under the weight of the toxic sludge covering him. "I should never have let those horrible boys and their talking pet anywhere near the plant. Can you hear me?"

"Yes, Daddy!" whimpered Randy and Mandy.

I'M SORRY BUT YOUR CHEESY BREAD LUNCH IS RUINED.

But strangely Mr Smugley didn't care about his lunch.

"We're all so very dirty," he said. "But I don't seem to mind – the sludge must be changing me..."

In fact, it was changing ALL of them because they were all enjoying feeling dirty.

"Yes, I actually feel quite good," said Mrs Smugley.

"So do we," said Randy and Mandy. "We like to be dirty."

"Yes," said Mr Smugley. "Forget antiseptic wipes – I like to be dirty too."

"Dirty is good!" continued Mr Smugley.

"Who cares if your lunch is dirty," said Mrs Smugley. "Let's eat it anyway!"

"Yummy!" said Mr Smugley.

"Isn't it?!" said Randy, grabbing a handful of the toxic sludge and throwing it at Lamby and Wamby. "Now let's make our pets dirty!"

"Nice!" said Mandy, throwing a blob of toxic sludge at the office floor. "Then let's make the floor dirty!"

"Let's make the walls dirty!" said Mrs Smugley.

"Let's make the computers dirty!" said Mr Smugley.

"Let's make the family car dirty!" said Randy.

"I've had enough of making things clean. From now on I want to make things dirty!" screamed Mr Smugley. "Let's make the whole world FILTHY!!!"

6 Later that week something almost as exciting as seeing the Smugleys getting sludged was happening at Gerald, Gene and Fleabag's school – the grand opening of a brand new, state-of-the-art toilet.

"But is it comfortable to ug-sleep in?" mused Fleabag – who we should mention lived in an old toilet at the end of Gerald's garden.

"I think it would be a bit too neat and tidy for you," said Gene. "Apparently, it's got a self-cleaning seat..."

"Not to mention a built-in digital radio, hot and cold toilet roll and even a back massager," added Gerald.

THE
DELUXBOG 3000
is the most modern, technologically advanced toilet ever built.
A combination of **space-age technology** and **cutting-edge luxury** make this the most pleasurable lavatorial experience
EVER!

But when they got to the toilet (which was hidden by a large curtain) there was already a huge crowd of excited kids gathered around.

"I'm delighted to introduce the inventor of the **DELUXBOG 3000**, Mr Finckle Flushgood," said Mr Troutman, the class teacher. "He will now say a few words before performing the grand opening."

Finckle Flushgood cleared his throat before addressing the school...

> For centuries, toilets have been horrid, dirty places. I wanted to change all that. So, I worked for decades, slaving away for years in my factory to make going to the toilet a cleaner, happier activity. And the result? The **DELUXBOG 3000**! It gives me great pleasure to declare my toilet open!

Mr Flushgood pulled the ceremonial toilet chain, sweeping the curtain away to reveal the brand new toilet. Everyone cheered and applauded.

"So, who's first?" asked Gerald. But the inventor himself was intent on being the first to use the spanking new toilet.

"You'll all have to wait your turn," said Finckle Flushgood, holding up a large book. "It's my toilet and I get to have first go!"

The door of the **DELUXBOG 3000** swooshed open to reveal a gleaming, shiny and thoroughly 21st century interior. Flushgood waved as the door shut behind him.

SWOOSH

"Typical," said Gene. "Why do *we* have to wait?"

"I'm ug-busting," said Fleabag.

And so everyone waited for Mr Flushgood to finish. And waited. And waited...

"I know he took a big book in with him," said Gerald. "But I didn't think he'd try to finish it..."

DELUXBOG 3000

But then something extraordinary started to happen. The walls of the new toilet began to shudder and shake – and then there was a ground-quaking roar that made the whole school judder...

"That's the loudest toilet flush I've ever heard," said Gene. "I wonder what's going on in there."

"This is not supposed to happen," said Mr Troutman. "The **DELUXBOG 3000** is equipped with another of Mr Flushgood's brilliant inventions – the world's quietest flushing device – the Hush Flush 360."

But as they waited for Flushgood to reappear even stranger things were happening at the sewage treatment plant. Let's find out what...

7 The Smugleys were now completely unrecognizable, their neat and tidy outfits in tatters. Instead they were filthy from top to toe and not only that but they were enjoying it! Together they headed off to find a dirtier place to be – **the sewers**!

"The time of cleanliness is now over!" boomed Mr Smugley. "It is a time for dirtiness! From now on we will be the **Royal Family of Filth**! I will be known as the Lord of All Things Sewage – the new ruler of the underground world – **King Pong**!"

Everyone cheered as he placed a crown made from a toilet plunger on his head.

"We want new names!" clamoured Randy, Mandy and Brandy. "And toilet plunger crowns!"

"And you shall have new names, and crowns," said King Pong. "Randy, from now on you will be known as ... the **Prince of Poop!**"

"I love it!" shouted Randy.

"And you, my precious Mandy," continued Pong, "will be known as ... the **Princess of Plop!**"

"I love it too!" cried Mandy.

"What about me?" said Mrs Smugley. "I want a name too."

"Well, you will be the First Lady of Dirt – from now on you will be known as the **Queen of Unclean!**" said King Pong.

"All hail, King Pong!" shouted the Prince of Poop.

"Long live the Queen of Unclean!" squealed the Princess of Plop.

"Glory be to Gross-Out!" boomed King Pong.

GROSS SAVE THE KING!!!

"Now it's time for me to tell you about my great project – **Operation Toxic Kingdom**," said King Pong. "We are finished with the clean world above. From now on we shall live here, in the sewers."

"Yes, it's so much dirtier down here," said the Prince of Poop.

"Who wants to be up there where people take showers?" said the Princess of Plop. "Yuck!"

"Indeed," continued King Pong. "But I want this to be a proper kingdom – with palaces, pleasure gardens and rat-drawn carriages – and for that we need a plan.
Let me explain...

"We are going to need people to join us down here to build our kingdom. And so I have devised a rudimentary toilet-sucking device."

"After people are sucked down the toilet they will be covered in the toxic sludge."

"This will make them lovers of filth just like us. They will be known as **Filthoids**."

"And the Filthoids will build us the grossest kingdom the world has ever seen!"

"What a fabulously filthy plan!" chortled the Prince of Poop.

"It's devilishly disgusting," added the Princess of Plop.

"I'm so proud of you!" beamed the Queen of Unclean.

"The only problem is that we need to speed up the process. We require an army of Filthoids!" said King Pong. "For that we need the assistance of the world's leading toilet scientist. And, if my calculations are right, he will be joining us any minute now!"

Back at school Gerald, Gene and Fleabag
had no idea about the existence of King Pong
or his plot. Right now concerns were growing
for the missing toileteer who had been locked
in the new lavvy for over an hour.

Gerald, Gene and Fleabag were already on the
case, examining the toilet from every angle and
checking out the locked door.

DELUXBOG 3000

"Mr Flushgood, can you hear us?" called Gerald
and Gene.

"I don't think I can ug-hold on much longer," said
Fleabag urgently. "It's my ug-turn!" But with no reply
it looked like more drastic action might be necessary.

"I think we need to break the door down!"
said Gerald.

"You can't break the school's beautiful loo," said Mr Troutman. "It's so shiny and new. Let me have a look."

But finally Mr Troutman agreed that there was no way in – they would have to enter the **DELUXBOG 3000** by force.

"But how are we going to do it? This door is made of reinforced steel..." he said, rattling the entrance.

"Fleabag can do it," said Gene. "Fleabag, time for some **Gross-Out Power**!"

"Ug-get down, everyone," shouted Fleabag. "Time for an ug-**turbo fart**!!!"

"Everyone look away!" screamed Gene as Fleabag bent over and let fly.

The door buckled and flew open...

But when the air cleared there was a loud gasp from the crowd – there no sign of Mr Flushgood! All that was left of the world famous lavatorial inventor were his shoes and the book he had been reading.

"This is strange," said Gene.

"This is very strange," said Gerald.

"This is ug- ug- ug-strange," said Fleabag.

"That's it," said Mr Troutman. "I'm calling in the industrial plumbers!"

As soon as they arrived, men with giant plungers set about the spanking new toilet.

"Be careful with the lavvy, you oafs!" fussed Mr Troutman.

"No sign of him," said the head plumber. "He must have been sucked clean away."

"Nonsense," said Mr Troutman. "He must be in there somewhere."

"How can a flush be that powerful?" asked Gene.

"It's not the flush..." said the plumber.

HE SEEMS TO HAVE BEEN SUCKED STRAIGHT DOWN THE SEWAGE PIPE!!!

9 Back underground King Pong's plot was advancing nicely.

"As you planned, we now have the world's leading toilet expert," said the Princess of Plop.

"At first he wouldn't co-operate," said the Prince of Poop. "But as soon as he was covered in toxic sludge he became very enthusiastic, and he's been hard at work ever since."

"Great! I can't wait to meet him," said King Pong.

The Queen of Unclean clapped her hands and a door opened.

A small, smelly-looking man entered the room. It was Finckle Flushgood, inventor of the **DELUXBOG 3000**! But gone was his shiny clean lab coat and in its place were filthy rags – he had become a Filthoid!

"Greetings, Oh Great Supreme Sovereign of Stink!" said the man. "I used to make lovely clean lavatories, but now I want to make everything dirty!"

"It is wonderful to have you on board the 'Good Ship Dirt'. From now on, you will be known as Mini-Muck," said King Pong.

"Oh! A special name of my own! Your generosity is remarkable, Oh Great Big Dirty One!" grovelled Mini-Muck.

"Aren't I wonderfully grubby?" purred King Pong. "How are the plans progressing?"

"Very well. I have used my extensive knowledge of toilet technology to increase the toilet-sucking side of the operation tenfold, Oh Glorious Overlord of Odour," said Mini-Muck proudly.

"That sounds wonderful," said King Pong.

"Yes, we are bringing people into the fold from all over town as we speak," said Mini-Muck.

"I have also speeded up the 'filthing' side of things," he continued. "With my new production line, people are sucked down the pipe, covered in toxic sludge and ready to be your loyal Filthoids in minutes!"

"This is fabulously mucky," beamed King Pong. "Soon we will have a Toxic Kingdom fit for the First Family of Filth!"

If you're finding this all a bit too gross, here is a picture of some butterflies having a tea party to make you feel better...

10 With Mr Flushgood working full-time recruiting Filthoids for the Toxic Kingdom, concerns were mounting as "toilet disappearances" became more and more common. Gerald, Gene and Fleabag, meanwhile, were in their favourite hangout, the **Gross-Out Den**. This was where they spent most of their spare time. It housed the Gross-Out Museum, and was where they could look at the filming they'd done for Gross-Out TV.

And it was also home to Fleabag Monkeyface!
In fact, the shed used to house the outdoor
loo and Fleabag's bed was the old toilet itself.

"Good thing this toilet was disconnected years
ago," said Gene. "It's the only safe WC in town."

"Well, I never ug-trusted that ug-minty clean
ug-Deluxbog," said Fleabag. "Anyone for ug-juice?"

"That would be nice," said Gerald nervously
– Fleabag's offers of food and drink were often
shockingly gross.

"Three ug-juices ug-coming up!" said Fleabag.

"Finckle Flushgood's toilet was state of the art,"
said Gerald. "How could someone vanish into it?"

Unlike the emergency services – who'd run out
of leads on the disappearing townsfolk – Gene was
about to have one of his famous "ideas".

"Have you noticed how quiet it's been around here
lately?" said Gene.

"Yes, it has been quiet," said Gerald.

"How no one has disturbed us in here..." said Gene.

"Of course!" said Gerald. "The Smugleys – we
haven't seen them in ages."

"Not since we visited the sewage treatment works,"
said Gene.

"I've got ug-orange or ug-apple," called Fleabag
from the back of the den.

"Er, apple," said Gene. "I've had an idea." We've
already mentioned that Gene always has the "ideas".

"I like the sound of this," said Gerald, who we've
also mentioned always liked Gene's "ideas".

"Well, you know where the pipes from the toilet
lead..." said Gene.

"Down the drain?" said Gerald.

"Yes, but after that..." said Gene.

"The sewage treatment plant!" said Gerald.

"Exactly!" said Gene. "I think something might be going on there. We need to make a return visit."

"Cool idea!" said Gerald.

11 As soon as Gerald, Gene and Fleabag got to the sewage plant, they realized it looked completely different from the last time they were there.

"Whatever happened to the neat, tidy pools and vats?" said Gene. "I would have thought Mr Smugley would have cleaned the place up by now."

"And what's this?" asked Gerald, looking at the green mucous-like substance covering everything.

"Ug-toxic sludge," said Fleabag. "Not even I would ug-go near this ug-stuff."

"So where are the Smugleys?" said Gene. "Let's try the office."

"There's no one here," said Gerald.
"But their car is still out there,"
said Gene. "They must have
gone somewhere ... but
where exactly?"

"Hang on an ug-second," said Fleabag, sniffing the air. "I can ug-sense something very ug-gross near by."

"Where's it coming from?" asked Gerald.

Fleabag had now sniffed his way out of the office to a nearby open manhole.

"Ug-here," said Fleabag. "Have an ug-look down there."

By peering down the hole the three of them could see an extraordinary scene unfolding in the sewers beneath them.

 **12**

"**Y**our new home is ready, Oh Wonderfully Whiffy One!" said Mini-Muck, unaware that they were being spied on. "The Filthoids have worked around the clock to build an abode worthy of the Royal Family of Filth!"

"What fantastically filthsome news!" boomed King Pong. "We must go there at once!!!"

"I can't wait!" simpered the Queen of Unclean.

"But King Pong – I like living in this dingy little sewer," said the Princess of Plop.

"Think how much filthier our palace will be, my delightful Daughter of Dirt!" beamed King Pong.

"Follow me," he said, and led them to the entrance of a massive pipe.

"But where exactly are we going?" asked the Prince of Poop.

"It is time to behold a realm made entirely of all things dirty – a realm of grand halls, palaces and a community happily living in filth, my beloved Son of Squalid... A place where only the filthy are welcome," said King Pong. "It is time for us to enter the Toxic Kingdom!!!"

13 As King Pong and his entourage vanished up the pipe, a great gate slammed shut behind them. Gerald, Gene and Fleabag had seen enough. It was time to act.

"It looks like your accident at the sewage plant has had large-scale implications," said Gene. "A toxic kingdom with people being sucked down the toilet and turned into Filthoids."

"I only wanted to ug-check out the gorilla ug-poo," said Fleabag.

"We're going to have to do something to stop them," said Gerald.

"We'll need to get a lot closer..." said Gene.

"How will we ug-do that without getting ug-noticed?" said Fleabag.

"I've had another idea," said Gene.

"Cool!" said Gerald.

"They're creating a kingdom of filth," said Gene. "The only way to get close to them is to be so dirty that we won't be noticed."

"You mean—" said Gerald.

"Yes," said Gene. "We need to disguise ourselves as Filthoids. It's time to get filthy!"

"Ug-great!" said Fleabag. "I ug-love to get filthy!!!"

"I was actually thinking about Gerald and me," said Gene. "You're filthy enough as it is. Now, follow me!"

First they went to Gerald's Uncle Stanley, a pig farmer, to get trousers. He was always up to his knees in manure, so you can imagine what his trousers were like.

Then they went to Gene's Auntie May, who kept pigeons, to borrow hats. The birds were always landing on her head so her hats were always filthy.

And, finally, they went to their classmate Darryl Fozz's house to borrow shirts. He was the messiest eater in school and his shirts were always covered in stains and bits of old food.

WE DON'T WANT ANY OLD SHIRTS...

BUT IF WE COULD JUST HAVE SOME OF YOURS, DARRYL.

With Gerald and Gene now top to toe in their dirty disguises the three of them were ready to meet King Pong.

"We've got Filthoid disguises," said Gerald, "but how are we going to get to King Pong?"

"Follow me," said Gene. "It's time to go to the toilet!"

14 Back at the sewage treatment plant, Gene led them to the office toilet.

"The ug-toilet!" said Fleabag. "Always a fun place to ug-hang out!"

"There's no time to hang out," said Gene. "We've got to save the world from filth."

"So, how does the toilet help us?" asked Gerald.

"We need to get to King Pong," said Gene. "That means going underground into the sewers where he's holed up."

"We need to get sucked down, like Mr Flushgood and all those other people," he continued.

"Cool!" said Gerald. "I've always wanted to meet a royal."

"Let's just hope that when we get underground we can track down Pong, Plop and Poop," said Gene. "Now we need to sit."

It was a bit of a squash but the three of them managed to squeeze onto the toilet seat. Where they waited...

And waited...

And waited...

Until...

SQUELCH!

The three of them were sucked down the toilet!

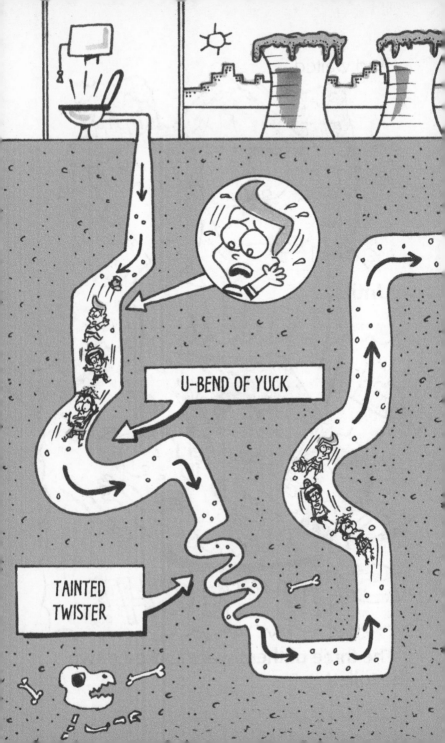

U-BEND OF YUCK

TAINTED TWISTER

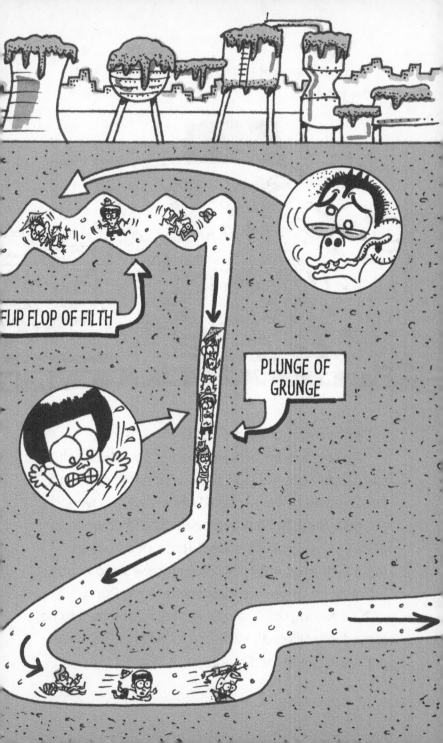

Then with a great splat they landed at the foot of the pipe.

"We're moving!" said Gerald.

"We seem to be on some sort of conveyor belt," said Gene. Sure enough, they were moving along a factory-style conveyor belt. Filthoids were covering the new recruits, who had been sucked down loos all over town, in toxic sludge. These people were instantly turned into Filthoids themselves and happily led away to serve their new master, King Pong.

"Quick, jump off!" said Gene. "We don't want to be turned into Filthoids. We need to infiltrate this place and track down the Smugleys..."

Meanwhile, King Pong and the Queen of Unclean sat on huge thrones. On either side of them, on slightly smaller thrones, were the Princess of Plop and the Prince of Poop.

"Behold the **Toxic Palace**!" boomed King Pong. "A palace made entirely of all things dirty!"

"It is a wonderful dwelling, Your Majestic Muckiness," said the Queen of Unclean. "So much filthier than the horrible, clean world above."

"It's grimier than we ever imagined!" said the Prince of Poop.

"A home fit for the First Family of Filth!" said the Princess of Plop.

"And the Toxic Kingdom and palace are only the beginning," said King Pong. "Mini-Muck, how are plans going for **Phase Two**?"

"Exceedingly well, Oh Supreme Ruler of Rot," said Mini-Muck proudly. "We will soon be able to unveil the pongiest plot ever proposed!"

"I can't wait," chuckled King Pong.

16 Gerald, Gene and Fleabag were about to discover the Toxic Kingdom for themselves. The three of them crept along the tunnel that led away from the filthing station.

"King Pong talked about a Toxic Kingdom," said Gerald as they crawled up. "But this looks like any old sewer to me."

"Where are the grand halls and the community happily living in filth?" said Gene.

"I don't know what you're ug-complaining about," said Fleabag. "This is my ug-idea of heaven – ug-sliding along a narrow ug-tunnel with ug-filth on all ug-sides!"

But even Fleabag stopped talking when they reached the end of the tunnel.

"This place is amazing!" said Gerald, looking around them.

"They have created a whole underground world," said Gene. "Populated entirely with Filthoids."

"Ug-wow!" said Fleabag approvingly. "This is my kind of ug-town! I need to go to the ug-shop, see a film at the ug-cinema then have a drink in the ug-cafe!"

"There's no time for that, Fleabag," said Gerald. "We need to get closer to King Pong to discover what else he's planning."

Fortunately, Gerald and Gene's disguises were so good that none of the Filthoids seemed to notice them.

"This is great," whispered Gerald. "We can walk among the Filthoids undetected."

"They're not taking any notice of *us*," said Gene. "But *Fleabag* seems to be getting quite a bit of attention!"

Fleabag was gross even by Filthoid standards and a small crowd had gathered around him. He was busy signing autographs!

"Sorry, Fleabag, we don't have time for your celebrity status," said Gerald. "We need to find King Pong."

17 It didn't take long for Fleabag to find out from a Filthoid where King Pong's palace was.

"We need to take an ug-right on U-Bend Avenue," said Fleabag. "Then a left on ug-Lavvy Pan Alleyway, then straight down ug-Skitter Lane to the ug-river."

"River?" asked Gerald.

"We need to take an ug-boat," said Fleabag. "The palace is at the ug-end of the River of Grubbiness."

After some negotiation (Fleabag agreed to have his photo taken with the head gondolier), they got into a boat and were heading downstream through an underground world made entirely of dirt.

...AND ON YOUR LEFT, YOU WILL SEE THE HANGING GARDENS OF MUCKYLON...

As they rounded a bend, Gerald, Gene and Fleabag almost fell out of the boat as vast portraits carved into the cliff-face loomed over them.

"They call that '**Mount Flushmore**'," said the gondolier.

And beyond the cliff lay the Toxic Palace. But before they could reach it, their boat was intercepted by a vessel carrying palace guards.

"What's going on?" whispered Gerald.

"I'm not sure," replied Gene. "Just act normal."

"There are rumours that rogue Filthoids may be attempting to smuggle soap into the Toxic Kingdom," said the Captain of the Guards. "King Pong will not tolerate any cleanliness. Unleash the sniffer rat..."

Straight away the sniffer rat scurried between passengers searching for soap, before stopping at Fleabag.

"I never go ug-near soap," he pleaded.

"Look – it's wagging its tail!" chuckled one of the guards. "That's the grossest thing it has ever seen. I'm sure King Pong would love to meet you and your friends!"

18 "Well, I suppose this way we get to meet King Pong," said Gerald, as they were bundled into the palace.

"Where ug-exactly are you ug-taking us?" complained Fleabag.

"To the throne room of His Royal Highness himself – King Pong," bellowed the guard. "And with him will be our beloved Royal Family of Filth."

Gerald, Gene and Fleabag were taken along corridors and up and down staircases until they were brought into a large hall. They were now up close and personal with the First Family of Filth!

"Well, if it isn't Gerald, Gene and Fleabag!" said King Pong, observing the new arrivals.

"Mr and Mrs Smugley! Randy! Mandy! What happened to you?" asked Gene. "You used to be so clean..."

"The Smugleys are no longer! The time of cleanliness is gone for ever!" cackled Pong. "Now I have established a Gross-Out Kingdom I want an Empire!!!"

"An Empire of Filth!" added the Queen of Unclean.

"And my head scientist, Mini-Muck, is ready to tell us the latest on our filthsome plan!!!" King Pong clicked his fingers and Mini-Muck entered the room.

"It's Finckle Flushgood!" said Gerald.

"That's Mini-Muck to you," said the toilet scientist.

"I have everything in place for **Phase Two** of our plan!"

"Soon everyone in town will have been turned into a Filthoid. But we need to spread our toxic sludge worldwide!"
"To do that we need a titanic toilet. And there is one on top of my toilet factory big enough to flush a vast quantity of toxic sludge."

"You'll never get away with it!" said Gene.

"Who's going to stop me?" boomed King Pong. "Guards, take these three to the deepest dungeon!"

"Can we keep the monkey creature as a pet?" begged the Prince of Poop. "He's so much filthier than Lamby and Wamby!"

"Oh yes, let us keep it," implored the Princess of Plop, skipping around and clapping her hands. "It's disgusting – but in a good way!"

"Very well," said King Pong. "But make sure you keep a close eye on him. I don't trust him..."

Before Gerald and Gene were led away by the guards, Gene managed to quickly whisper to Fleabag. "Play along. We'll give you the signal when we're going to try to stop them..."

19

The next two days were terrible for Gerald, Gene and Fleabag.

Gerald and Gene found themselves in the most disgusting underground dungeon.

But for Fleabag it was even worse – he was now the Smugleys' plaything!

They dressed him up as **Little Bo Poop** (their favourite nursery rhyme). Lamby and Wamby were the sheep, of course.

They made him play **Pass the Plunger**.

They made him join in their silly games, like **Pin the Tail on the Donkey's Dirty Bottom**.

They even made him take part in their **family singalongs**.

ROW, ROW, ROW YOUR BOAT GENTLY DOWN THE SEWER

THE HANDLE ON THE LOO GOES FLUSH, FLUSH, FLUSH

Gerald and Gene needed a plan, and fast!

"The only place we can stop King Pong is above ground," said Gene. "We've got no chance down here – there are guards everywhere."

"How are we going to get him above ground?" asked Gerald.

"When he goes to the Flushgood Toilet Factory," said Gene.

"And how are we going to get past those guards?" asked Gerald.

"We aren't going to escape," said Gene. "We're going to be invited along."

"Invited along?" said Gerald incredulously.

"I've had another idea," said Gene.

20

"This had better be good," said King Pong, lounging on his throne. "I don't usually grant private audiences to prisoners. I'm a very busy monarch – I have an empire to build, you know. Besides, the Princess of Plop and the Prince of Poop are entertaining us all with a game of monkey tennis."

Over King Pong's shoulder, Gerald and Gene could see the prince and princess playing with Fleabag on a court of filth, with a pair of Pong's underpants for a net.

"This is marvellous!" squealed the Queen of Unclean. "Monkey Wimbledon is *soooo* much fun."

As Fleabag was forced to play tennis with his new masters, Gene spoke to King Pong.

"We would like to be there for your finest hour – the global sludging at Flushgood's Toilet Factory," said Gene.

"What and give you the chance to escape?" chortled Pong. "Take them back to the dungeon – they are wasting my time..."

"We would like to *film* it!" said Gene, just before he was grabbed by guards.

"Film *me*?" said King Pong, his eyes lighting up. "I'd forgotten about Gross-Out TV."

"Yes," said Gerald. "To preserve your finest hour for ever."

"It would be a smash hit," continued Gene. "Playing in cinemas worldwide—"

"With me as the star!" gloated Pong. "And my family could also have prominent roles!"

"I've always wanted to be a movie star," said the Queen of Unclean.

"You would all be wonderful," said Mini-Muck. "Perhaps I could have a small walk-on role?"

"I don't think so," said King Pong. "You can arrange the camera equipment. Now take them back to their cells – we leave this afternoon."

"My plan is working," whispered Gene. "I knew they wouldn't be able to resist the chance of being in a film."

"Yes, but what are we going to do when we get to the toilet factory?" asked Gerald urgently.

"I'll tell you when we get there," said Gene. "But we're going to have to get Fleabag away from the Smugleys – we're going to need a massive dose of **Gross-Out Power**..."

With their brand new film gear Gerald and Gene joined the royal party as they made their way underground to beneath the Flushgood Toilet Factory.

"We are here, master," said Mini-Muck. "Above us is my factory and on it is the world's largest toilet."

"I have a huge vat of extra strong toxic sludge," he added. "Enough to filth every sewage pipe in the world."

"Good," said King Pong. "I want a quick dose before I go – I need to be **super-toxic**."

King Pong smeared himself in some of the extra strong sludge ... and once again he began to change.

SHLURP!
DOLLOP!

SUPER TOXIC
SLUDGE

22 "I hope my plan works," whispered Gene, before addressing the super-sized King Pong. "We need to go ahead to get in position to film you."

"Very well," said Pong. "But no funny business."

"We need Fleabag to come with us," said Gene. "We need him for the filming. He's our ... er ... sound engineer."

"Sound engineer?" said King Pong. "Mmm. So be it, but when you're done, my children want him back. They have become very fond of the little beast..."

Gerald, Gene and Fleabag made their way up
a nearby pipe and back above ground.

"Thank ug-goodness you ug-got me away from
those horrible ug-brats," said Fleabag. "I couldn't have
ug-taken another ug-minute with them."

"Well, if my idea works, you'll never have to be
their pet again," said Gene.

"What is your idea?" said Gerald. "If it doesn't work
the whole world is going to go toxic."

"Follow me," said Gene. "We need to get
into position on the roof of the building next to
Flushgood's – it will make sense when we get there..."

"The only way to stop King Pong is by creating the world's biggest chemical flush," said Gene. "And Fleabag – *you're* going to be the flusher!"

23 But before Gene could explain the rest of the plan, the Flushgood Toilet Factory began to rumble and shake.

"I think Pong is about to make his entrance," said Gene.

"And his horrible ug-children," winced Fleabag.

RUMBLE
RUMBLE

Sure enough, a now colossal King Pong appeared in the giant toilet bowl. On his shoulder was the vast vat of toxic sludge, and perched on top of that was Mini-Muck. The Prince of Poop, Princess of Plop and the Queen of Unclean lurked behind him, applauding and cheering his every move.

"THE TIME HAS COME TO MAKE THE WHOLE WORLD TOXIC!!!!" screeched King Pong, before looking over in the direction of Gerald, Gene and Fleabag, and adding, "Are you getting this?"

"Quick! Pretend to film," whispered Gene.

"NO MORE SHOWERS, NO MORE SOAP!" Pong continued. **"SOON YOU WILL ALL LIVE UNDERGROUND IN FILTH WITH ME!!!"**

I'M UG-READY TO RUMBLE!

"Make sure you get my good side!" he added, looking at Gerald, Gene and Fleabag again.

"Yes, Your Mucky Majesty!" replied Gerald as he pointed the camera in the direction of King Pong. "This is going to thrill audiences globally!

"Great work, Gerald – you keep King Pong busy posing!" said Gene, before turning to Fleabag. "We don't have much time..."

"We need a huge bottle of toilet detergent," he continued. "Enough to flush away King Pong and his family for good."

"Where are we going to ug-get that?" asked Fleabag.

"It's right here," said Gene, pointing at the huge advertising bottle erected above them on the roof of the detergent factory.

"I need you to **turbo-fart** with that bottle to above the toilet," Gene added. "Then use a **supersonic sneeze** to release the detergent over King Pong."

"Time for ug-**Gross-Out Power**!" yelled Fleabag, before springing into the air. He turbo-farted the bottle off its stand.

"Then we can flush King Pong and the Filthoids away, for ever!" said Gerald.

TURBO

FART!

Fleabag was directly over King Pong but before he could unleash the detergent, King Pong started to swipe at him.

"What are you doing?!" he screeched. "You're meant to be the sound engineer. Get away from me!"

Fleabag ducked and hovered, trying not to lose his balance.

"Don't let him open that bottle," wailed Mini-Muck. "We must not be exposed to clean, fresh detergent!"

With Fleabag out of reach and about to open
the bottle, King Pong's family tried to let the bloated
monarch know what was going on.

"He's right above you!" wailed the Princess of Plop.
"You've got to stop him!"

But King Pong turned his attention to Gerald and
Gene. Reaching out he snatched them from the
roof of the detergent factory.

"So, you thought you could trick me into
being covered in detergent!" he screeched.
"Time to call it a wrap! Filming is over for
you three – FOR EVER!!!"

"Let us go, you horrible pile
of yuck!" replied Gene.

"You've ruined our
film gear *again*,"
said Gerald.

"Hit them with some toxic sludge!" screamed the Prince of Poop.

King Pong grabbed a great handful of toxic sludge and hurled it at Fleabag. But Fleabag repelled it with a volley of **supersonic bogeys**!

"Now, Fleabag!" shouted Gene.

"Let him have it!" added Gerald.

But before Fleabag could unleash the detergent, King Pong fixed him with his gaze and spoke in a warm, friendly voice.

"Stop! Think!" he cooed. "Why don't you join me?"

"Ug-join you?!" said Fleabag.

"Yes, join me," said King Pong. "You could be my right-hand man. The toast of the gross-out world... Just think, you and the Royal Family of Filth ruling over an Empire of Gross..."

Forget the Gross-Out Den...
You could have a whole sewer,
just for you!

THE FLEABAG MONKEYFACE
**SUPER–DUPER
SEWER**
VIEWING BY APPOINTMENT ONLY

You could have a **hundred chefs**, all preparing the mos rotten and putrid foods for you on a daily basis...

"And would I have a special name?" asked Fleabag dreamily.

"Yes, you would be the **Earl of Hurl**," said Pong. "So, come on, put the detergent down and let's get on with filthing the world."

"Fleabag, no!" shouted Gene. "We know you love gross-out, but this is wrong."

"But we could ug-make the whole ug-world gross..." said Fleabag.

"We like the world as it is," said Gerald. "It's more fun when most people like things nice and clean but we're a bit different. If everything was gross it would be boring..."

"Come on, Fleabag, put the detergent down," said King Pong. "Don't make me demote you."

"We need to get through to Fleabag before it's too late," whispered Gerald.

Then Gene had his best idea so far.

"Fleabag," he said. "I've got two words to say to you."

"Ug-what?" said Fleabag. "I'm a busy ug-right-hand man, you know."

"**Monkey tennis**," said Gene.

It worked! As memories of his humiliation at the hands of the Smugley twins flooded back, Fleabag turbo-sneezed open the bottle of detergent and poured it on the crowd below.

"Ug-never again!" he cried.

"Help! Horrible clean stuff!" wailed King Pong, releasing Gerald and Gene. "I'm getting smaller!"

"Our lovely dirty outfits are being ruined," moaned the Queen of Unclean.

"It's counteracting the toxic sludge!" warned Mini-Muck as he desperately tried to shake off the detergent.

"We're melting!" cried the prince and princess.

"Now **FLUSH**!" bellowed Gene.

With a final effort, Fleabag tugged the giant flush with all his might. There was a loud gurgling noise as water and detergent poured down on King Pong and his cronies.

"We're being swept away!" said Pong.

"You've done it!" cheered Gerald, as they clung onto the rim of the giant toilet. "You saved the world from a toxic sludging!"

"Let's go to the sewage treatment plant," said Gene. "I hope the detergent reached every corner of the Toxic Kingdom..."

25 Gerald, Gene and Fleabag made their way back to the sewage plant as quickly as possible, and when they got there they couldn't believe their eyes. People in rags were staggering out of the plant – the Filthoids were free!

"Looks like the detergent worked," said Gerald. "Everyone is back to normal."

"I think they need a shower!" said Gene.

"Ug-yuck!" said Fleabag.

Finally, a wretched-looking group appeared – King Pong, the Royal Family of Filth and Mini-Muck were out of the sewer and above ground.

"What happened to us?" wailed Mr Smugley. "We actually liked being dirty... I need antiseptic wipes, now!"

"It was like a horrible grubby nightmare," sobbed Mrs Smugley.

"I can't believe we actually touched that thing," whimpered Mandy Smugley, pointing at Fleabag.

"And poor Lamby and Wamby – will you ever forgive us?" snivelled Randy.

"I need to get back to making nice clean toilets," croaked Finckle Flushgood.

26 With the Smugleys back to normal and the world saved, Gerald, Gene and Fleabag were back in the Gross-Out Den.

"Shame about our film," said Gerald. "It would have been great on Gross-Out TV."

"At least people can go to the loo without worrying about being sucked into the Toxic Kingdom," said Gene.

"To think I was ug-tempted to join King Pong," shuddered Fleabag, going to make snacks.

"That was a close call," said Gene.

"Yes, it's great that everything's back to normal," said Gerald. "The Smugleys are back to being annoying, we're back in the Gross Out Den..."

"And Fleabag's no doubt preparing us something really gross to eat," said Gene.

But when Fleabag returned something was seriously wrong... Something much more alarming than King Pong, something much scarier than an army of Filthoids... Fleabag was wearing a neat cardigan and had a flower in his hair.

"Who's for ug-fairy cakes?" he asked. "Or a nice ug-fresh fruit salad? I'll just ug-leave these here, I need a nice ug-wash. Anyone got ug-bubble bath?"

To discover what's happened to Fleabag, you'll need to read the next "Disgusting Adventure of Fleabag Monkeyface" – which makes this one look like a fluffy, clean flannel with pictures of kittens on it. **Don't say we didn't warn you!!!**

If you can't wait until the next
Fleabag Monkeyface book, here's
a free comic to keep you going.
(It makes perfect on-the-toilet reading!)

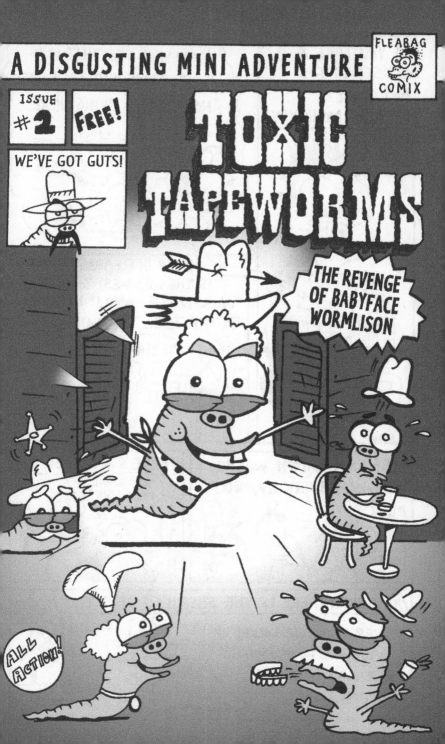